THE FAMILIAR'S WINGS

THE PARANORMAL COUNCIL #7

LAURA GREENWOOD

Visit Laura Greenwood's website at:

www.authorlauragreenwood.co.uk

Cover Design by Ammonia Book Covers

The Familiar's Wings is a work of fiction. Names, characters, places, and incidents are the products of the author's imagination or are used fictitiously. Any resemblance to actual persons, living or dead, businesses, companies, events, or locales is entirely coincidental.

The Familiar's Wings was previously published as *Spellbound*.

A second chance at love makes sparks fly…literally.

Ethan was left heartbroken when his childhood sweetheart, Eliza, moved away at seventeen. Now, fate has brought them back together, and Ethan is determined to make her work for his forgiveness.

Eliza has always regretted leaving Ethan, even if she'd have had to hide her true nature from him if she'd stayed. But once they come together again, they learn things about one another that they'd never known before.

CHAPTER ONE

ELIZA WALKED THROUGH THE DOOR, grateful to be home after a horrendous day at work. She'd graduated from university the year before, and had been lucky enough to get an entry level marketing job for a well-known clothing brand. And she hated it. A lot of her job was tedious, but she hadn't known what she wanted to do when she finished her degree, so had settled on what she was best at.

She waved her hand towards the kitchen, a bright blue spark leaving her fingertips, animating a chopping board and knife. The day her Mum had taught her to use her magic for cooking, had been one of the best of her life. Before that, she'd been made to cook by hand, which just made using magic all the better. She'd known she was a witch since she was a little girl, but her powers hadn't manifested until she reached eighteen. For some reason, witches either developed magic while they were still toddlers, or when they reached adulthood. At first, Eliza had resented being one of the late bloomers, but seeing the havoc her younger sister, Camille, had caused, she'd finally decided that it was a blessing in disguise.

A chirping noise came from behind her, and a small smile crossed Eliza's face.

"Hey, Bluebird," she crooned at her familiar. All witches had one, though very few would ever be seen by other people. Bluebird had appeared to her after she'd been left alone on her eighteenth birthday, thankfully after she'd got a basic grip on her new powers. Much like Eliza's normal magic, Bluebird was made of blue sparks, and yet, she didn't seem to be controllable in the same way. Bluebird appeared when she wanted to, and did what she wanted to, making her more like a low maintenance pet than magic.

Eliza poured herself a glass of white wine, having learnt from experience that there were a few things that magic couldn't, and shouldn't, take care of. There'd been too many liquid related accidents for her to trust her powers with pouring.

Eliza jumped at the sound of her phone ringing, and she made the mistake of answering before checking who it was; not that it would really matter. The only people who were likely to call her were her parents, or her eighteen-year-old sister.

"Hello," she said, taking a sip of wine.

"Hi Liz," a deep male voice sounded at the end of the line.

"Todd," she greeted. Eliza sighed inwardly, dreading the conversation to come. She wouldn't deny that she'd been attracted to Todd the first time they'd met. He was tall, dark and handsome personified, and just her type. It'd been her type ever since her first boyfriend in high school. It didn't hurt that he had one of those deep and sexy as sin voices either.

The only problem with Todd was that she'd become bored. It seemed to happen a lot with the men she dated, not that there had been many of them. At first, she'd be totally into them, especially if they reminded her of Ethan. Unfortunately, that soon seemed to wear off. Often even before they had sex.

"You free tomorrow night?" he asked.

"I'm not sure, I'll have to check." She cringed at the fact she hadn't just told him no, but she hated telling men she wasn't interested. A quick glance at her dinner told her it was almost time to put it in the oven; another job that she'd discovered was better done without magic. Unfortunately, the distraction didn't take long enough for Eliza's liking.

"Well?" Or it took too long, according to Todd.

"I'm sorry Todd, I promised Camille I'd go ice skating with her." She crossed her fingers, hoping that he wouldn't be able to sense a lie. Really, she shouldn't be worrying about that, but it was habit from growing up in a paranormal household.

A lot of paranormals were able to sense lies, especially if they were told by someone close to them. Which meant that she was probably safe from plain old human Todd.

"Seriously? Can't you cancel?" The whine in his voice made Eliza grit her teeth. He was fast becoming as annoying as he was boring. It was definitely time for her to get rid of him for good. Heartless though that may be.

"No, I can't. Bye, Todd." She hung up without waiting for a reply, and hoped that he got the message. They'd only been on three dates, which was two more than Eliza should have gone on. She'd known that he wasn't the one for her after the first date. Though why she'd ever thought that was the case was beyond her. She was a witch. Her 'one' was most likely a paranormal being of some kind.

Sadness flowed through her, just like it did every other time she thought about her 'one'. Somehow, she'd got through her string of boring men without losing her romantic streak, and there was still a part of her that mourned the loss of her high school boyfriend. But like the others, Ethan had been just human, and her family moving away had been a blessing in disguise.

She'd been the one to break it off between them, and she'd done so with tears streaming down her face and her heartbreaking. She'd loved him then, and it had been difficult to do, even if her Mum had tried to persuade her that she'd get over the adolescent infatuation with time. Eliza wasn't convinced. There was still a part of her that loved him, and probably always would. After all, there was a reason that all the men since Ethan looked just like him.

She tried to change the direction of her thoughts, otherwise she'd just end up feeling worse when she remembered that she'd never see him ever again. Or that Ethan had just been human, and that there wouldn't have been any future for them anyway. It always hurt to think about that, and she suspected that she'd never truly get over him. Whatever that meant for her future. Maybe she was one of those people that would end up alone forever. She probably deserved it after what she'd done to him.

CHAPTER TWO

ETHAN SANDERS HATED MONDAYS. Though he did wonder if there was anyone that actually liked them. If he was completely honest though, he hated every day, and had done ever since the love of his life had moved away. It wasn't a very manly thing to admit, but when it came to Eliza, he didn't care; nor had he ever. Even if she wasn't a witch, like he was, there was just something about her. Everything, from her long dark hair, to her no-nonsense attitude was perfect to him. She'd always been sure of who she was, and no one had been able to persuade her differently. He'd always admired that about her.

The day that Eliza had ended it between them was branded on his mind, no matter what he did. Even the nights getting drunker than he'd ever thought possible hadn't helped. The night she'd broken it off, she'd been visibly upset, and had even gone as far as saying she didn't want them to end. He'd tried his absolute best to persuade her they could still be together; he'd been sure that long-distance would work. In hindsight, he knew that he'd been wrong. Not that he doubted Eliza was meant to be his; he was still certain about that despite the heartbreak. Rather, he doubted either of them would have been happy with a long-distance relationship. At least this way he'd had some semblance of his own life, even if he'd never found anyone to replace her. He doubted he ever would.

He took a sip from his coffee, only to almost spit it out. It seemed that he'd been too engrossed in his graphic design project, and had let it go cold. He glanced around the office to make sure that no one else was around, before cupping his hands around the mug and sending his power into it. Red sparks crackled, and the coffee began to steam again. Ethan smiled to himself; sometimes being a witch had its advantages.

He turned back to his screen, concentrating on the design he was working on. The brief had been frustratingly exact on what the clothing company wanted. On the one hand, he supposed it made his life easier to have such a clear vision to work to. On the other, it was frustrating to have such a precise set of rules and not let his own creative flair have a say. A nudge came at his hand, and he looked down, shocked to find his familiar, Flame, sat there and pushing his head against Ethan's skin. The magic sparks he was made of tickled a little, but Ethan was used to them and they didn't bother him.

Ethan still found it odd that Flame was a bird. From the hints his family had given him over the years, most of them had feline familiars. And familiars tended to run in families. Yet, on his eighteenth birthday, despite it all, up had popped the little bird made of red sparks. Not even his family knew that his familiar was different. Ethan had never outright lied to them about it, but neither had he told them. Even if he wasn't sure what it was, there would be a reason for Flame's appearance. One day, maybe he'd even discover what it was.

"Hey, buddy. What're you doing here? You'll be seen if you're not careful." To most people, it would probably seem odd that he was talking to what was essentially a collection of magical sparks, but as far as he could tell, it was actually a fairly normal thing for witches to do. Though he'd never actually seen another witch with their familiar to know that for sure. The secrecy surrounding such an important part of witch culture was perplexing at times. Ethan tried not to think about it too much, or he'd invariably end up with a headache.

Flame nudged his hand again, before pointing his beak towards the right-hand side of Ethan's computer screen. Ethan glanced over and was surprised to find that it had already gone eleven, meaning he'd been here at least four hours longer than everyone else. He jumped to his feet, careful not to spill his almost empty coffee in the process. Normally it didn't matter how late he worked, it wasn't like there was anyone waiting for him at home, and his hours were logged via his computer anyway, so there was no risk of being underpaid. But tomorrow was different. He had a meeting with the client he was working for, and while they'd probably just send some poor soul who was too far down the pecking order to be able to say no, Ethan still wanted to be alert for it.

Plus, there was something in his gut telling him that tomorrow's meeting was even more important than it should be. He didn't actually have any precognitive powers, though he'd heard that some witches did. That kind of thing also tended to run in families. But, over the years, he'd learnt to trust his gut instinct, and if it was telling him that tomorrow was going to be important, then going home and having a fairly decent night's sleep was probably the best idea.

CHAPTER THREE

ELIZA HAD A FEELING ABOUT TODAY, and while she didn't know where the feeling had come from, she spent extra time getting ready all the same. She even styled her hair, something that she barely ever did, even if it would only take a wave of her hand to do. It wasn't that she didn't like to look good, but more that she figured that there were more important things in life.

Her hair now fell in natural-looking waves, much like her everyday look, but a little sleeker, and it completed the look she'd gone for. Her electric blue satin shirt brought out her blue eyes, and the pencil skirt suit she'd teamed it with was the perfect combination of business and sexy, providing the confidence boost she needed. She still wasn't sure what she needed that confidence for, but at least it would help her to get through the meeting she had today.

It'd been foisted on her by her superiors, and considering her low-down position within the company, she hadn't been able to avoid being the one to go. It wasn't likely that she'd have said no anyway, she wasn't confrontational enough for that.

The trip to the office took a mere fifteen minutes, during which, butterflies had made themselves at home in her stomach. She wanted to scream at them, and tell them to get lost. It was just a normal day at work, and the meeting was a simple check-up to see that the graphic design company was doing what they should be, nothing more. She tried to give herself a talking to, and was grateful that she was alone in the car, or else she'd end up looking crazy. Not that was a new thing, she talked to herself all the time. She got caught all the time too, but she didn't want to risk looking any crazier than she already did.

Eliza logged herself into the meeting room she'd booked, and powered up her laptop. She was determined to get some work done while she waited, especially since the other people in her team spent more time gossiping than they did actually working. It made getting on with things a shade more difficult. She was busy typing away when the phone in the middle of the conference table rang, making her jump. She really should work on being less spooked by ringing phones.

"Hello?" She propped the phone between her shoulder and her cheek, continuing to type as she did.

"Miss Davidson, I have a Mr Sanders here to see you," said the voice at the other end. She was only half-listening, and she barely registered the name of the man she was meeting. It wasn't like it mattered anyway. The design company hadn't named her contact, and she suspected that the man was just a lackey like she was.

"Okay, I'll be with you in a few moments." She saved the document she was working on, and pushed back her chair. Slowly, she made her way through the brightly lit corridor and down to the ground floor. "Hi, Denise." She smiled brightly at the ageing receptionist who seemed to be a permanent fixture on the front desk.

"Hi Miss Davidson, he's just over there." Denise pointed to a tall, dark-haired man, who was examining the display of mannequins, each wearing clothes from one of the company's ranges.

She'd never admit it out loud, especially not while she was at work, but Eliza would never be caught dead in any of it. It was far too faddy for her.

This morning's weirdness aside, Eliza normally wore comfortable clothes; jeans and t-shirts on the weekend, if not her pyjamas, and equally as comfortable work clothes. With the occasional suit skirt if she had an important meeting.

Denise leaned forward and made a come-hither gesture, a conspiratorial look on her face. Humouring her, Eliza leaned forward.

"Just wait until you see his front," Denise said as she winked. Eliza gave her a fleeting smile.

"What did you say his name was again?"

"Mr Sanders," Denise replied, only half paying attention to Eliza. The rest of her attention was focused on the man's rear. Eliza didn't blame her; it was quite something to look at. But this time, when Denise said his name, it registered, and she began to look at the man in a completely different way. The man turned around, and caught her staring, not that it was enough to stop her doing it. Nor did it stop her heart hammering in her chest, while simultaneously dropping like a stone.

While she hadn't seen him in nearly six years, there was no doubt in Eliza's mind that it was Ethan standing in front of her. He had the same dark hair and brown eyes, with the intense gaze that he'd had for years. Except that he was broader now, and without a doubt, he was manlier. At school, he'd been on the rugby team, but he'd been that position that the skinny boys who happened to be able to run fast played, she'd never been able to remember what the position was called. If he still played, then she was sure he'd now be part of the scrum.

Her mouth almost began to water as she took in the sight of him in dark trousers, and a smart white shirt open at the neck. He had a suit jacket slung over his arm, but like her, he'd probably decided that it was too hot outside to wear it. She didn't blame him; it was unseasonably warm for early May, and it felt like it was getting hotter in reception by the second.

Ethan stared back at her, clearly giving her the same appraisal that she'd given him. Much to Eliza's disappointment, he was the first to break free from the spell. He strode forward, closing the distance between them and offered her his hand. She looked at it, unsure if taking it was a good idea. It had been years, but she wasn't naïve enough to believe that he wouldn't still affect her. Even with space between them, she could feel the tension building. It'd always been like that with them.

"Hi, I'm Ethan Sanders," he introduced himself, as if they were strangers. But she noticed the slight curl of his mouth and the glint in the eye that often accompanied his playful moods.

"Eliza Davidson." She took his hand, and the moment their skin touched, what felt like a bolt of magic travelled through her. Maybe she was imagining it after the shock of seeing Ethan. That was by far the most logical explanation. At least, she figured that was more likely than their touch causing a magical reaction. Surely she'd have noticed it while they'd dated before.

The two of them lingered over the touch, which probably looked odd from where Denise was sitting. Thinking of the receptionist, Eliza hastily pulled her hand away and gestured towards the lifts. "If you'd like to follow me."

The moment the lift doors closed, and the two of them were alone, Eliza could almost swear that the magic sparks were back, except this time they weren't even touching. She tried to dismiss them as a mere hallucination, but nothing she was doing or thinking would make them go away. She briefly considered actually using her magic to attempt to make them disappear, but quickly shut down that notion. She couldn't do that in front of a human, even if the human was Ethan.

"It's good to see you," Ethan said, breaking the silence the moment that they were in the meeting room.

"You did recognise me then?" Eliza cursed

inwardly, hating just how awkward her question had sounded.

"How could I not?" he muttered, setting down his bag and pulling out a tablet. He sat down in one of the chairs and made himself comfortable. She could feel his dark brown eyes watching her, but rather than feeling uncomfortable or objectified, Eliza found herself appreciating the attention. It'd been too long since any man had made her feel like that.

"How've you been?" She was at a loss for what to say. Technically, she supposed that she could have started the meeting. After all, that was the real reason he was here. But something in Eliza thought that it was a bit rude to do that, especially when they hadn't seen each other in so long. Also considering that she'd pretended more than one of her lovers had been him.

She shook her head slightly, desperate to rid herself of the images her imagination had conjured up. When they'd dated as teenagers, they'd only ever had sex the once. It'd been the night before she'd moved, and they'd never had a chance to repeat the experience. But her overactive imagination had plenty of fun conjuring up images of things they could have done together. Particularly when she was feeling unsatisfied.

"I've been good. What about you?" he answered.

"Yeah, alright thanks." They lapsed into silence. "I've missed you," she blurted out without meaning to. She cursed herself, it wasn't that she'd lied. More that it wasn't the kind of thing she wanted to admit in front of an ex, even if it was true. A slow smile spread across Ethan's face, making him appear all the more handsome to her.

"I've missed you too," he admitted, surprising her. She smiled back, and the two of them took the opportunity to move on to the work that they were supposed to be meeting about, the awkwardness banished by the safe subject.

She quickly discovered that he was good at his job, and had easily taken what she'd thought of as an overly controlling and dated brief, and turned it into something wonderful. He'd even managed to get it so that the graphics would actually appeal to teenagers. That could only be a good thing, considering they were the company's target market. Though they wouldn't know for sure until the idea had been put in front of a test group. The groups seemed to have a lot of power around here, and she'd seen more than one concept destroyed when they went in front of one.

She watched as Ethan packed his bag back up, enjoying how his shirt stretched over his back as his arms moved. He turned back to her, just in time to catch her staring, and smirked at her.

"Didn't anyone tell you that it's rude to stare?" She smiled back at him, remembering when she'd said those exact words to him the day they'd met. He'd been staring at her from across the playground. They'd been nine, and she'd just moved to a new school. Which had happened a lot during her childhood. In fact, the eight years they'd spent in Ethan's hometown had been a long time for her family.

"Nope, must have missed that lesson," she replied. Ethan laughed, a deep sound that went through her in a thrilling way. That's what he'd said to her that day too, and just the memory was enough to make her heart feel lighter than it had in years. At first, they'd just been friends. It wasn't until they were at high school, at fifteen, that they'd started to look at each other in a different way.

"Would it be too much to ask if we could hang out?" she asked him, before she could bottle out. The laughter fell from his face, and a more serious look replaced it.

"Eliza…"

"Just as friends," she cut him off. She had no way of knowing what he'd been about to say, but the look on his face was enough to convince her that it wasn't good. And now that she'd seen him again, the thought of not having him back in her life was making her feel oddly uncomfortable.

"I'm not sure I can be just friends with you." His voice was soft, almost like an apology, but her heart latched on to what he'd said, noting that it wasn't actually a no.

"A non-friend, non-date, dinner then?" she asked nervously. She hadn't realised quite how much she still wanted him until that moment. Except that wasn't actually right. She'd known for years, she just hadn't wanted to admit it. It wasn't great to have to admit that she was still pining over someone she hadn't seen in six years.

"I don't know, Eliza. I'm not sure I can," he said, a pained look on his face. Almost as if he didn't really want to say the words. Her heart sank, and she questioned whether this really was the end for them.

It wasn't like they'd broken up because either of them had done anything wrong, surely there could still be something there. He must have seen something in her expression, because he sighed and pushed his hand over his face and through his hair. The gesture left the dark strands sticking out in all kinds of directions and gave him the sexily mussed look that many men would pay good money for.

"Can I think about it?" It might not have been the

answer that she was hoping for, but at this point, Eliza was willing to take what he could give.

"Sure," she agreed with a nervous smile. She gave him one of the business cards she kept in her bag, making doubly sure her mobile number was on it. She'd changed her old one as soon as her family had moved away, not trusting herself enough not to call Ethan and stop them both moving on.

"I'll text you." He leaned forward and kissed her on the cheek, branding her like he had the first time. It was that moment that Eliza realised that she had no hope of ever truly being over him, and that she realised she would do almost anything to win him back.

CHAPTER FOUR

THE CARD in his pocket hadn't strayed far from his mind for the rest of the day, and it had taken everything Ethan had not text her already. Almost as much effort as it had taken not to pull her into his arms and kiss her senseless. The outfit she'd decided to wear hadn't helped. He'd wanted to rip it off her, or better yet, magic it away. He shook his head, determined to remove the inappropriate thoughts.

The moment he'd seen her looking at him, he'd forgotten almost everything that was important, and he could have sworn that his heart had skipped a beat. He'd always wondered if he'd see her again, but now that he had, he was surprised by the strength of his reaction.

Eliza had always been physically beautiful. Even

as a nine-year-old, he'd been able to appreciate her as being pretty, but it was more than that.

Just so long as Ethan remembered not to let her reappearance cloud his judgement, he'd be fine. As much as he'd love to let her back in and pick up where they left off, she'd broken his heart, and there was a part of him that was still hurting over it. He wasn't ready to forgive and forget quite yet.

Flame flickered into life the moment he walked back into his small flat. Not that it needed to be any bigger. He'd only moved in a week ago, having finally had enough of the student area he'd lived in previously. The late-night parties he'd had to listen to almost nightly, had finally got too much for him. He'd chosen to live alone and, while he could have roomed with another witch, that would have limited the times that Flame was about. Which was as good a reason to live alone as Ethan could think of, there was something comforting about Flame's crackling presence. He'd always wondered if the bond he felt with Flame was the same as what other witches felt for their familiars, but it was a taboo subject, so he'd never know.

He wasn't even sure why familiars were such a no-go, but whenever he'd asked his parents about it, they'd shared a secret smile that made him think that it was something to do with mating. Ethan frowned, realising that mating was another part of witch society that was shrouded in mystery. He didn't even know how mating worked between two witches, or even if they could mate quite like other paranormals did. It was alright for shifters and vampires, they could just bite their lover, but with witches that just wouldn't work. And not just because the idea of biting anyone was a little bit repulsive for him.

Ethan shrugged off his jacket, throwing it over the arm of his sofa. He pulled his phone out of his pocket and stared at it, trying to decide if texting Eliza was the right thing to do. His heart was telling him yes, just like it had been all day, but his head was reminding him about what happened last time.

He knew that, technically, their break up hadn't been Eliza's fault, but at the time it had felt like the rug had been pulled out from under him, and that his world would never be the same again.

A knock sounded at his door, surprising him and making Flame disappear with a faint pop. Ethan shook his head; familiars were funny things. He'd never understand how they worked. He strode over to the door, swinging it open and stopping dead when he saw who was standing on the other side.

She was drenched. Her long dark hair dripping water onto her shirt, making it stick to her in a way that really wasn't helping Ethan stay in control.

From the look of surprise on Eliza's face, she hadn't expected him to be on the other side of the door either.

"Ethan..." she trailed off, looking somewhat uncertain. He wasn't sure why. After the initial awkwardness of seeing him again earlier, she'd come across as the confident woman that he'd known she'd become. Eliza Davidson knew exactly who she was, and she owned it. She always had. And yet, for the second time today, she looked lost for what to say. "I'm sorry, I didn't know you lived here." She turned to go, but Ethan grabbed for her hand, shocking them both this time.

"Eliza, you're soaked. Come in and dry off at least." It took her a moment, but she stepped back through the door, and into the warmth. Ethan let go of a sigh of relief. He knew having her here was dangerous, especially for his sanity, but he couldn't let her go back out in the rain.

"I'm sorry, I locked myself out, I only live next door," she told him, before he had a chance to ask her why she was here. He was disappointed that she hadn't made the trip just to see him, but then again, he'd only just moved in. Up until today, he'd had no idea who his neighbours even were. He supposed that he could have made her wait in the hall, but that still seemed cruel.

"I didn't realise you lived here either," he pointed out uselessly. His nerves getting the better of him.

Eliza's bright blue eyes locked on to his, and the two of them stood in silence, unable to look away. Finally, Ethan pulled away, knowing that if he looked at her any longer, he was going to do something stupid; like kiss her.

"Do you want a coffee?" he mumbled, desperate for something to do with his hands. Especially if it meant that he could leave the room.

"Sure. Is it alright if I call the landlord while you make it?" She motioned with her phone, which was clasped in her right hand. He nodded once.

"Black with one sugar?" Her eyes widened and he mentally kicked himself. He wasn't sure why he'd said that, and didn't like that it revealed just how much he remembered about her. It had been six years. That should have been enough time to forget. At least, that's what he told himself every time he started to think about her again.

"Yes," she answered weakly. She fiddled with her phone, and he walked into the kitchen, at a complete loss for what to say to her. Ethan busied himself making drinks, and tried his best not to listen in on her phone call. He knew that she was only calling their landlord, but it still felt wrong to invade her privacy.

A familiar crackle of electricity sounded, and Ethan was surprised to see Flame flicker into life beside the kettle, his bright red sparks almost glowing in the dim lighting. He hadn't bothered with the main light, there was no need when he had smaller ones already on.

"You can't be here," he hissed at his familiar, throwing a worried glance back at the living room. Thankfully, Eliza was still making her phone call, hadn't come looking for him. Flame chirped quietly, but didn't vanish, only confusing Ethan more. The familiar shouldn't be around at the moment, and normally he wouldn't be. If even a fraction of what he'd been told about familiars was true, then Flame shouldn't have appeared until after Eliza had left his home.

"Ethan?" Eliza asked, but didn't come into the kitchen. He threw a stern look at his familiar, before carrying the drinks back through to her, unable to quite shake the uneasy feeling caused by Flame's appearance.

CHAPTER FIVE

SHE HEARD Ethan coming back through from the kitchen and shooed Bluebird away with her hand. She wasn't sure why her familiar had appeared, particularly in a new place and with Ethan so close by, but she couldn't risk Bluebird being seen. The last thing she wanted was the very human Ethan asking questions she didn't know how to answer. She didn't even know if humans could see familiars. She assumed they could, but then, they tended to be unobservant at the best of times. It was amazing how many shifters got away with wandering around in animal form without humans noticing. Just this morning she'd seen a blue jay that was ever so slightly bigger than the norm, and almost certainly a shifter in disguise.

"Here you go," Ethan said, handing her a coffee.

She wrapped her hands around it, enjoying the warmth. She really should remember to put her umbrella in her handbag. It'd save accidents like today.

"Thank you."

"What did he say?"

"Huh?" Eliza hated to admit it, but she was completely distracted by the smell that seemed to be coming from Ethan. It was a mix of coffee, spice and something completely his own. It was a scent that she'd tried to forget, but would recognise in an instant. His smell was simultaneously exciting and comforting, it always had been.

"The landlord, what did he say?" he asked, surprisingly unflustered, given the circumstances. If he'd turned up on her doorstep, completely soaked and unannounced, then she wouldn't have been impressed. Actually, that wasn't true. If it had been the other way around, she'd have suggested he take his clothes off so she could dry them for him. Eliza's mouth went dry just thinking about that. She only had her memories, and her imagination, to go on, but she reckoned naked Ethan would be a sight to behold.

"Sorry," she answered after a moment too long. "He'll be here in an hour or so. I can go grab a drink somewhere else if you prefer..." she trailed off, aware of the coffee in her hand. She also didn't want to leave unless she had to.

"No need, you can stay here."

They stared at each other for a long moment, neither moving an inch. Electricity crackled through the air, building the tension between them. Or at least, that's what it felt like to Eliza. Her eyes kept straying down to his lips, and she could almost feel them pressed against her own. She had to wonder whether their first kiss in years would be soft and sensuous, or rough and passionate. Looking at him now, she hoped for the latter; she wanted nothing more than to rip his clothes off, preferably with her teeth. She supposed that she could just make them vanish with magic, but that might raise uncomfortable questions. Although, maybe she could make his shirt catch on something. Might still be hard to explain, but shirtless Ethan would be totally worth it.

Ethan cleared his throat, bringing her out of her heated daydreams. She took a sip of her coffee, surprised to find that he'd made it exactly how she liked it. Her heartbeat quickened as she began to hope that he was still as fixated on her, as she was on him.

"Thank you," she muttered. Ethan fidgeted uncomfortably, the spell now broken.

"So…"

"I think Abra Cadabra is on." She shrugged. They'd loved that show when they were younger. She still loved watching the amateur magicians battle it out, as well as trying to spot if there was a real witch in the mix.

"You still watch that?" He looked surprised.

"Every year," she admitted. Sure, it was a bit stupid, but it reminded her of him, and she was a glutton for punishment. Without saying a word, Ethan moved over to the TV, switching it on and pulling up the channel. Which made Eliza wonder how he knew where to find it. He sat down on the sofa, and set down his mug on the table in front of him, then motioned for Eliza to join him. Reluctantly, she sat down next to him, nervous to be this close to him, and itching to touch him.

"I don't think Stacey's going to last," he said with a smirk. She caught him giving her a sideways glance and gently swatted his shoulder.

"And you questioned me watching it."

"I couldn't very well admit it, could I?" This time, he turned to her, a mischievous sparkle in his eyes.

"You're right though, she won't," she said. The magician in question had a habit of fumbling tricks. At the moment, the public vote was keeping her in, but there was always a stage in the competition when the voters seemed to start taking it more seriously. That's when Stacey would go. "Now Brad…" Ethan laughed, cutting her off.

"You're just saying that cause he's hot."

"Am not!" She only realised after she said it, that she'd responded too quickly. Blood rushed to her cheeks and she looked away, slightly ashamed to have been caught being so shallow. Ethan smirked, proving he didn't believe her, but not saying anything.

Despite the earlier awkwardness, they watched the rest of the show in relative comfort. Just like they had when they were younger and the show had first come out. If she remembered right, and she was sure that she did, it had first started showing when they were fifteen. It had been while they were watching the show that they'd shared their first kiss; a clumsy and innocent one looking back, but at the time it had almost set her world aflame.

Eliza's blood began to heat up again, or at least it felt like it did, and she tried her best to ignore how close Ethan was to her. And how good he smelled. To make matters worse, the urge to do magic was building up within her. She frowned, unsure about what was going on. It'd been years since she'd gained full control of her powers, and she shouldn't be experiencing a build-up like she was.

The lights flickered, and she jumped slightly, causing Ethan to chuckle. "Scared of the dark Liza?" Excitement flooded through her as his use of her old nickname registered, but she pushed it away.

"No."

Ethan quirked an eyebrow in amused disbelief and she burst into a fit of uncontrollable giggles. It took mere moments for Ethan to join her. Their laughter ran its course, leaving both of them panting for breath. The muscles on Eliza's face were sore from smiling too much. She caught the look in Ethan's eyes, and shivered. It was almost enough to make her forget that they had any history together.

The tension mounted, and without even realising what she was doing, Eliza leaned towards him, barely aware that he was doing the same himself. The moment their lips touched, something long dormant exploded inside her. No wonder the other men she'd dated hadn't lasted; not one of them had made her feel like this with a simple kiss. Ethan's hand moved to the back of her head, cradling it at the same time as pulling her towards him. Meanwhile, Eliza's hand tightened on his shirt, desperately trying to hold on. She didn't want the moment to end.

She wasn't sure which of them initiated it, but she somehow ended up lying back on the sofa, with

Ethan above her, and their kiss still unbroken. Without really meaning to, she pushed her hips up towards him, craving more and not caring if he knew it. From the feel of things, she wasn't the only one.

They broke apart briefly. They stared into each other's eyes, neither wanting to break the connection.

"Ethan," Eliza whispered hoarsely. He smirked slightly, but didn't lose the glazed look of lust in his dark brown eyes. He dipped down, crushing his lips to hers, searing her skin and causing the crackling electric sensation again. The lights flickered around them, but Eliza didn't notice; she was too consumed in what was going on between them.

Ethan's hand tugged urgently at where her shirt was tucked into her skirt, and she lifted her hips again in an attempt to help him. Before she quite knew it had happened, her shirt was on the floor, and Ethan was peppering kisses down her neck. Eliza moaned low in her throat, unable to stop herself.

Power crackled around Eliza's fingertips, and it took her a moment to realise what was happening. Quickly she pushed Ethan away, causing him to fall onto the floor with a loud thud. She glanced down at her hands, shocked and worried to discover that blue sparks were still circling around them. She glanced quickly at Ethan, who'd stopped rubbing his head and turned to look at her, a strange look in his eyes.

"I can explain," she started.

"You're a witch," he spoke over her. She stared at him, not sure how to respond. He shouldn't even know what a witch was, never mind that she was one. Even more worryingly, he should be freaking out right now, but instead, a wide smile spread over his face. "You're a witch!"

Ethan jumped to his feet and pulled her up from the sofa, enveloping her in a tight hug.

"Ethan?" she asked cautiously. She wasn't too sure what was going on. He set her down slowly, the large grin still in place. Instead of saying anything, he held out his hands towards her, red sparks that matched her own dancing around them. Eliza's eyes widened as what he was showing her sunk in. "How didn't we know?" she whispered.

"When did you develop your powers?" He sat down on the sofa, pulling her with him and scooping up her shirt from the floor. He handed it back to her, which was when she noticed that it was still fastened down the front. Unbuttoning it, she realised that he must have used his powers to take it off, only she'd been too distracted to notice. She closed her shirt, glad to be covered for the conversation to come.

"Eighteen," she murmured.

"Maybe that's why." He tucked a stray strand of hair behind her ear, his hand lingering, and a compassionate look in his eyes.

"About what happened…"

"It was always going to happen."

She smiled at that. Even since before she'd seen him again, Ethan had been the man she thought about, and that included when she'd been in bed with other men. Which meant that she'd had very little doubt in her mind that something more would happen between them. But he'd been so adamant earlier that he needed time, she thought it would take a while to wear him down.

"I know what I said earlier, but there's something about you, Liza."

"But why didn't we know about each other?" Ethan shrugged.

"Secretive families, I guess."

"And when we slept together, I hadn't actually developed my powers. So, no light show." She gestured to her hands. Ethan chuckled.

"No, no light show."

"It didn't hurt, did it?" She worried her lip between her teeth, concerned about the effect her powers may have had on him. While he was a witch too, and was likely just as accustomed to magical accidents as she was, she still couldn't shake the fear that her powers had hurt him.

"No, it was actually rather pleasant. Once I realised what was happening."

Eliza cocked an eyebrow at him, and he turned so she was facing her properly. A smile pulled at the corners of his mouth as the red sparks surrounded his fingers again. He reached out, and gently trailed his fingers down her arm. Almost instantly, Eliza felt a tingling sensation, unlike anything she'd ever felt before.

"Ethan," she almost whimpered. He leaned in, not moving his fingers from her bare skin. Eliza's phone rang, making both of the jump and fall about laughing.

CHAPTER SIX

ETHAN LISTENED as Eliza took the call from their landlord, silently glad that it sounded like the man wouldn't be coming any time soon. He didn't think Eliza would leave after what they'd just shared, but he'd never been able to second guess her. There was a little part of her that was too free-spirited for that, even if she hid it well. She'd looked drop-dead gorgeous in her business suit earlier, but now, with mussed up hair and her clothing in disarray, she was sex personified. At least, she was to Ethan.

On a whim, he slipped his arms around her waist, stopping her from pacing the room. He pulled her back to his chest and her breathing hitched. Ethan chuckled, careful to be quiet so that the landlord on the other end of the phone couldn't hear him.

Dipping his head, he began to trail kisses down her neck, and felt her pulse begin to race in response.

"I'm sorry, I'm going to have to go." She squeaked as she finished speaking, making Ethan smile against her skin. She hung up the phone and threw it onto the sofa, turning around in his arms. "That was mean."

"Was it?" he teased. "Tell me he can't come tonight."

"Nope, he can't come until tomorrow." She smiled back at him and Ethan's world stood still. No matter what he told himself about making her work to win him back, he loved her, and had for years. There was no way that he was letting her go now.

Eliza's hands flew to the top of his shirt. He hadn't long been in from work when she'd arrived, and hadn't changed out of his work clothes yet. Deftly, she unbuttoned his shirt, pushing it down his shoulders and into a puddle on the floor.

"Would this not be easier?" he asked and summoned his magic, picturing their clothes on the floor with his shirt. It took more concentration than he really had, but he managed to leave the two of them standing there, just in their underwear. Ethan breathed in sharply. At seventeen, mostly naked Eliza had been beautiful, especially to a seventeen-year-old guy who'd never had sex before. Now, she was so much more. Her breasts weren't the biggest, but they were perfectly in proportion to the rest of her, or at least, they were if Ethan's ideas were anything to go by. Then again, he'd judged every woman he'd ever been with by Eliza, so it wasn't surprising that she was perfect.

He could feel her eyes on him too, and subconsciously puffed out his chest. He'd filled out since the last time she'd seen him naked; a combination of getting older, and spending more time at the gym to work off some of the frustration he felt. Not for the first time, he was grateful that he wasn't a shifter. He'd heard that they had to work out a hell of a lot more just to keep on top of pent-up energy.

Eliza raised her hand and drew it down his chest, a thoughtful look crossing her face. Her hands lit up with pale blue sparks, and she continued her exploration, sending shivers down Ethan's spine. While her use of magic earlier hadn't been unpleasant, the unexpectedness of it had meant that Ethan hadn't had a chance to really enjoy it. Now that she was using magic on purpose, Ethan could appreciate that it was like nothing he'd ever experienced before. It made him wonder why witches never spoke about using magic like this, but he pushed the thought away. There was a chance that what was making it feel so good was because he was with

Eliza for the first time in years. He didn't care either way.

Her hand trailed lower, pushing beneath his boxers and taking him in her hand. Ethan tipped his head back, trying to bite back a groan. The combination of her hand, and the magic surrounding it, was almost more than he could take.

"Liza, you're going to have to stop."

"Am I?" she asked in a teasing tone. He looked back at her to see a twinkle in her eye and a mischievous smile on her face. But despite her words, she let him go, causing both relief and disappointment to flow through Ethan. "Sit." She pointed to the sofa, and he followed orders immediately. He didn't know what she had planned, but from the look on her face, he was bound to enjoy it.

She waved her hand in his direction, this time removing the last remaining clothing from their bodies. She didn't give him long to admire him, as she slinked forward and straddled him. She pressed her lips to his in a searing kiss, which he couldn't help but compare it to the first, and last, time they were together. Last time, there'd been a lot of fumbling and trying to work out what went where, the lack of which almost made Ethan sad for the years that they'd lost.

"Stop thinking," she murmured into his ear,

giving it a sharp nip. Ethan groaned low in his throat, not wanting her to stop. She took him into her hand again, and stroked slowly, this time without the sparks. It probably took too much concentration for her to be casting magic right now. He knew that he probably wouldn't be able to do any himself right now. Though later, once they could take their time, he was eager to see what they could do with it.

Slowly, she slid down onto him, making both of them stop breathing for a moment. There was something so right about the feeling of being in her, like nothing else could make him feel so complete. Ethan locked his arm around Eliza's back, drawing her to him as she began to move, sending a bolt of desire through him. If this was anything to go by, he wasn't going to last long.

They moved in unison. Neither of them saying anything, or able to do anything other than whimper and grown. Ethan could hear that Eliza's breathing was as heavy as his, but was unable to focus on anything more than the feel of her skin against his. Each moment between the two of them was electrifying and ground breaking.

A familiar tightening sensation came over Ethan, and he knew that he wasn't going to last much longer. Thankfully, Eliza didn't seem able to hold on either, as she tightened around him, her whimpers gaining in volume and making it increasingly difficult for him to hold back. He thrust into her faster, and cried out the moment she did. Blue and red sparks erupted from their bodies and entwined together around them, but neither of them were paying much attention. At least they weren't until the lights flickered, and the room was plunged into darkness.

The two of them collapsed onto the sofa, still locked in each other's arms. After a moment to catch their breaths, they burst out laughing. Ethan almost couldn't believe that they'd managed to cause a power cut.

CHAPTER SEVEN

ELIZA STRETCHED OUT, and was disappointed to find that she was alone in the bed. It seemed like they'd only tripped the fuse the night before, as the lights had come back on after a few minutes. It was only then that they'd been able to move, and made the short trip into Ethan's bed. Which was where they'd spent the rest of the night, exploring each other in ways they'd never had a chance to when they were younger.

No matter what, Eliza would always cherish the memory of their first night together. They'd both snuck out of their houses, and met each other in the woods. It'd been summer, so still warm, and Ethan had brought a blanket and picnic with him. They'd both drunk a little bit of champagne, snatched from Eliza's family stash, and then they'd plucked up the courage to do what they'd wanted to for months. It had hurt a bit, but Ethan had gone slowly, as unsure about what he was doing as Eliza had been. The next day, she'd had to leave, and it had broken her heart almost as much as it'd broken Ethan's.

A chirping sound brought her back from her bittersweet memories, and she looked up to notice Bluebird whizzing around, desperate to get her attention. Eliza held out her hand, and her familiar landed on it, much smoother than a normal bird would have done.

"What are you doing here?" she stage-whispered, even though she knew that the bird would only respond to her in chirps and whistles. One thing that had always baffled her about familiars, other than their secretiveness, was that they didn't actually seem to do anything. Not that she didn't appreciate Bluebird, because she did. She liked knowing that there was always someone around for her. But she wasn't sure exactly what they did. The only viable theory she'd ever come up with was that the familiars were linked to their magic in some way. "Bluebird, you can't be here," she repeated.

Ethan's footsteps sounded outside the room, and Bluebird vanished the moment he stepped through the door, laden down with what appeared to be a breakfast tray. Regret filled Eliza as she realised all that she'd missed out on when she'd left Ethan behind. She could have had years of mornings like this, instead, all she'd had was lonely alarm clock calls and awkward mornings after.

"Yours giving you a hard time too?"

"What?" she responded instantly, confused by what he meant.

"I heard you talking, and guessed it was to your familiar." He shrugged, and sat down on the bed, resting the tray between them. Eliza immediately picked up the mug closest to her and took a drink, enjoying the perfect cup of coffee. Now that she knew Ethan was a witch too, she had little doubt that magic was one of the reasons he could make such good coffee, especially if he'd been able to use it since he was a child. She briefly felt a spike of jealousy about having to wait until she was eighteen to develop powers, but squashed it down quickly. It was hard to have negative thoughts about a man who brought breakfast in bed.

"Yes, she's getting bold. She normally doesn't appear outside my flat." She picked up a slice of toast, being careful to eat it over the tray and not get any on the dove grey bed sheets. They weren't what she'd have imagined Ethan's bedding to look like, but the neutral colours suited him. Or they suited the Ethan that she used to know.

"Flame is too. I wonder what's up with them."

"I'm not sure, it's almost like she wants to be spotted by you," she said.

Ethan didn't say anything either, probably because he was thinking the same as she was. There was an often-dismissed rumour that familiars could only ever be seen by two people; their witch, and the witch's partner. Or mate, or true love. Eliza wasn't actually sure what it was even called for witches.

"Bluebird," she said softly, wondering if summoning would work. Crackles sounded and the two of them watched in awe as the bird sparked into life.

"She's a bird," he said softly. Eliza couldn't read the expression that accompanied the words.

Ethan held out his hand, and Bluebird hopped along and onto his palm. Slowly, he stroked the bird's head, and it chirped happily. He looked up, and opened his mouth as if to call his own familiar, when something whooshed past Eliza's face and came to rest on the bed near Ethan's hand. And that was when she understood the look on Ethan's face, and was sure that it was now mirrored on her own.

His familiar was almost identical to hers. Except that his was made up of red sparks, like his magic, and ever so slightly bigger.

"This is Flame," he introduced, in what was a

slightly surreal situation, even for a witch. Introducing someone to a familiar just wasn't done.

"Hi Flame." The familiar hopped up to her, much like Bluebird had done to Ethan, and nuzzled into the palm of her hand. "But why?" She was almost too afraid to ask the question, but knew she had to.

"I have a guess." He looked at her, an emotion in his eyes that she was too scared to name. She waited for him to speak again. She had her own ideas about what he was going to say, but she needed to hear it from him first. "I think it's something to do with mating. Eurgh, that's an awful word," he said, pulling a face. Eliza giggled despite herself.

"Why don't we go with bonding instead?" She wasn't sure where the suggestion had come from, but something about it seemed right. Maybe she'd overheard her parents talking about it when she was younger.

"I like that," he replied with a smile.

"So, you think we're meant to bond?" she asked slowly, weighing up what that meant for the two of them as she did. Ethan picked up the tray and put it carefully on the bedside table closest to them, before slipping back onto the bed and crawling up to her. She leaned back, but even so their faces were mere inches apart. Not that she was complaining, his dark eyes and pre-shave stubble were a serious turn on.

Not to mention the fact that he'd only put on a pair of pyjama bottoms when he'd got out of bed earlier, allowing her to see every inch of his toned chest.

"I think we already are." He nuzzled into her neck, sending shivers down her, and making her arch up into him. Their bodies slotted together so easily, that there was no way she could dispute what he was saying.

CHAPTER EIGHT

IT FELT like he was walking on air, or at least that was the only way he could think of to describe how he was feeling. Despite previously telling himself that he wouldn't just forgive Eliza if he saw her again, and then completely disregarding that the day he did, he didn't have any regrets. He'd always known that there was something special about her, and the last couple of nights had only proved that. While they hadn't managed to cut out the lights again, the physical side of their relationship was only getting better.

But that wasn't what had Ethan feeling so good. Instead, it was the little things; like watching her use magic to change the colour of her shirt that first morning. The landlord hadn't turned up to let her into her flat, and she'd needed to get to work. He was still in disbelief that she was a witch. Even if he'd seen her use magic too many times in the past few days for it not to be true. It'd surprised him how quickly the two of them had become comfortable using magic in front of each other in so little time; especially when he'd spent his whole life hiding it from anyone but his family. Though he was first to admit that he liked feeling at ease about magic.

Even stranger still was the way their familiars were acting. From the moment the two of them entered a room, both Flame and Bluebird whizzed around, chattering away in whatever language they communicated in, while completely ignoring the two witches. Which was fine by him. It gave him more time to spend with Eliza.

"Hey bro." Ethan's friend, Lukas, clapped him on the shoulder, making him jump. He'd been too engrossed in his thoughts of Eliza, and what they'd been doing the night before, and hadn't been paying attention to his surroundings. Plus, he was nearly at work, and he never ran into anyone unexpectedly around here.

"Everything alright Luke?" he asked with a frown. He wasn't sure why Luke was here, and it was very unlike him to turn up unannounced at the best of times. The fact that he was outside Ethan's work, just days after a life-changing event, made Ethan wary. Even if Luke was his best friend, and the person that had picked up the pieces of him after Eliza had left the first time.

Luke was the opposite of Ethan in almost every way, down to his insistence that everything be done in a specific way. Growing up, Ethan had pulled a lot of pranks on Luke, particularly once he'd gained a better control over his magic. Even now, he still found it funny to move anything that Luke set down. And it annoyed Luke just as much now as it had all those years ago.

"I've been trying to call you for three days," Luke admonished him, a stern look on his face. Ethan cursed silently. He hadn't been paying any attention to his phone. He'd had no reason to. Luke was the only person who ever called him anyway, and his friend hadn't been the first thing on his mind since Eliza's return.

"Sorry, I've been busy."

"She must be pretty special to have distracted you that much," Luke sneered. Anger rose up inside Ethan, and tell-tale tingles began to surround his hands. Ethan took a deep breath, knowing that the street was not the right place to start accidentally start firing off magic.

"It's Eliza," Ethan told him, keeping his face as

impassive as possible, and watching as shock, and then disgust, crossed over his friend's features.

"That bitch?" Luke spat out, surprising Ethan with the venom in his voice. "She broke your heart Ethan. And you've just let her back in as if she did nothing wrong? She must be one hell of a lay." It took all Ethan had not to punch his friend there and then, but he knew that Luke was only trying to look out for him.

"It's not like that. It wasn't her that made them move away and you know it."

Luke gave him a sceptical look.

"What is it about her?"

"She's the one, Luke."

Luke's sceptical look turned into a frown, but Ethan didn't care. Whether Luke liked it or not, Eliza was back in his life, and this time, she was here to stay.

"Don't tell me you believe in all that shit," Luke said, not sounding impressed with Ethan's choices. "It's not real Ethan, don't let the woman fool you."

It was Ethan's turn to frown. He knew that Luke wasn't exactly a romantic. Really the opposite was true, and if Luke was anything, then he was a bit of a player. One who had a different girl every week. Most of them were drop dead gorgeous too; models that he met through his job as a photographer, for the most part. Ethan had tried to be jealous of Luke a few times over the years, but he'd never been able to force the emotion. Maybe it was because he'd already met Eliza, and his heart was too tied up in her to appreciate other women.

"What did you want, Luke?" Ethan asked, having calmed himself down. He checked his watch as if to accentuate his point, though his office was suitably laid back that being late wouldn't be an issue, especially considering the amount of overtime he did. He was hurrying Luke along more so that he didn't have to spend too much longer on the subject of contention.

"To take you out for your birthday."

That stopped Ethan for a moment. He'd completely forgotten that his birthday was coming up, and that it was a tradition for the two of them to go out drinking and dancing. Or at least it had been once they'd turned eighteen, before that, Ethan had spent his birthdays with Eliza, even if Luke had been his friend longer. Normally there were also some failed attempts to pick up women, or at least on Ethan's part there had been. Luke had never seemed to have a problem with it. At least this year, he wouldn't have to worry about that.

"Sure, how's Friday?"

"You're not going to ditch?"

"I promise I won't ditch." He was almost hurt that Luke felt the need to ask, but then again, he probably would ditch if Eliza asked him to. It was a good job that Eliza wasn't high maintenance.

"And you won't bring her?" Venom dripped from Luke's tone as he said the last word, making Ethan wonder what this was really about. Eliza and Luke had got on fine when they were younger, or at least they had as far as Ethan had known. Maybe they'd just been pretending for his sake, though he hoped not.

"I won't bring Eliza." He stressed her name as much as he dared. He'd have to work on Luke once they'd had a few drinks on Friday night.

"Good," Luke said, a smug look on his face. He turned, waving once behind him as he did. Ethan rolled his eyes, not knowing what else to do. He shot off a quick text to Eliza, explaining about Friday night. They hadn't had any plans, but he still didn't want her to be disappointed. Shutting down his phone, he turned and made his way into work, not looking forward to the day ahead.

CHAPTER NINE

ELIZA CURSED herself for giving in and coming out tonight. When she was with the right people, she loved going out drinking and dancing just as much as the next twenty-something. But Ethan had told her he was out tonight, and not having any other plans, she'd managed to get herself dragged on to a work's night out. She couldn't say that her idea of a good night was seeing Mary, the older lady who managed one of the accounts, squeezed into a bright turquoise halter dress that was at least two sizes too small. Or listening to Delilah, who did almost exactly the same as Eliza did, singing at the top of lungs, not to mention terribly off-key. If she'd had her way, and she couldn't spend the evening with Ethan, then she'd much rather spend it curled up with in front of the TV.

"Hotty alert," Delilah said loudly. Eliza felt guilty for being relieved that the singing had stopped. Delilah pointed towards a tall, dark, and broad man leaning against the bar, making Eliza's heart sink. The last thing she needed was Todd around. Even though she'd told him it was over, she'd received a barrage of texts from him in the past couple of days, and she doubted that her silence had made the message any clearer to him; even if it should do.

Slowly, Todd turned around, and eyed up the women looking at him. When he caught sight of Eliza, his eyes took on a predatory glint and she shivered; she really didn't want to have to deal with Todd. There'd always been something a little off about him, more than just the fact that he wasn't Ethan. And the last thing she wanted was to get on his bad side and discover exactly what that off thing about him was. If only she'd listened to her gut instinct and not dated him in the first place; but she'd been lonely, and he'd looked enough like Ethan to fill the void.

"Let's get a drink," Eliza half-shouted over the loud music, grabbing Delilah's hand. She attempted to pull the other woman towards the bar at the opposite side of the dance floor, and far away from the one Todd was standing at. But Delilah wouldn't budge, her eyes locked on Todd stalking towards them. Eliza wasn't sure how she could tell, but she knew that his eyes were locked on her and not the woman next to her, and she found the sensation rather disturbing. She was at the point of leaving, when she realised it was too late. There wasn't a massive amount of space between where they were and the bar that Todd had been standing at, but there was enough that it should have taken longer for him to get to them than it seemed to have. Maybe she'd let the alcohol affect her more than she'd meant to. She'd never had the same level of control over it as most paranormals.

"Eliza," Todd half growled.

"You know him?" Delilah asked, her words running together in her excitement.

"Unfortunately," Eliza muttered darkly, but far too quietly for either of them to hear. Especially over the noise in the club. Despite that, Todd smirked, almost as if he'd heard.

"You've been ignoring me," he said. Eliza refused to acknowledge the comment.

"Delilah, this is Todd. Todd, Delilah. Have a nice night." She plastered on a fake smile and attempted to slip away, only to be stopped by a tight grip on her wrist. She tried to break away, but he was surprisingly strong; almost too strong for a normal human. "Let go." She glared at him, and he chuckled darkly.

"Not a chance," he said, not loosening his grip.

"How do you two know each other?" Delilah asked, oblivious to the undercurrent of tension between Eliza and Todd.

"Now, Todd," she demanded, hoping he'd let go of her wrist this time. She felt bad for ignoring Delilah, but it had to be done. She wasn't comfortable with this situation, and didn't want the other woman involved. Especially as Delilah was just human, not to mention likely to get hurt if she was caught in the crossfire. Which actually gave Eliza an idea. She glanced around quickly, to make sure that no one other than Todd and Delilah were paying any attention; Delilah was drunk enough that she probably wouldn't remember what was about to happen, and if Todd said anything, then it would just be his word against hers.

Summoning up her magic, she focused on where Todd had hold of her wrist, and let the sparks go. She felt the jolt of magic travel from her skin to his, but nothing else happened. She frowned, and began the process again, summoning more magic this time and hoping for a bigger shock.

"That's not going to work, little witch," Todd sneered, making Eliza's blood run cold. If he knew what she was, then that meant that he probably wasn't human either, and that she hadn't been able to tell. Worryingly, that left very few options for what he really was. And as far as Eliza knew, none of those options were good news for her.

Todd turned to Delilah, but his grip on Eliza's wrist still didn't loosen. Eliza could tell that he was doing something to the other woman, but couldn't make out what, especially as he wasn't making a sound. Which ruled out him being a necromancer at least. And considering the rumours going around about them, that was probably good news for Eliza.

Delilah's eyes glazed over, and she turned away from the two of them and wandered off into the crowd. Relief washed through Eliza as she realised that her workmate was at least safe from whatever was going on now.

Someone grabbed hold of her around the waist, taking her by surprise, and lifted her up easily. Eliza tried to kick and scream, but nobody seemed to notice. Todd was looking around him now, and the crowd were gaining the same dazed look as Delilah had a moment ago. Which meant only one thing; he was a vampire. And an old one at that. She'd heard rumours that only the oldest could successfully perform mind control. Not that any of that would help her, only other paranormals would be unaffected, and most of them would stay out of it. Even if they heard her scream.

CHAPTER TEN

THE MOMENT he heard the scream, Ethan knew that something was desperately wrong. To make matters worse, something in his gut was telling him that it had a direct impact on him. Mere seconds later, both to his and Luke's surprise, both Flame and Bluebird appeared in front of them, whizzing about frantically. If the club had been quieter, he was sure that he'd be able to hear the twittering away. He exchanged a worried look with Luke, his heart sinking as he realised what the familiars' appearance probably meant.

"Oh, hell no," Luke said after seeing the look on Ethan's face. But this time, Ethan wasn't going to stand for it.

"She's in trouble, Luke."

"How could you possibly know that?" his friend growled back.

"That is her familiar." He pointed sharply at Bluebird. "Do you think she'd have appeared in front of you, or the rest of the people here, if everything was alright?"

"And she wouldn't have a problem appearing in front of you?" Luke seemed sceptical, as Ethan guessed he had every right to be. This wasn't normal in the slightest.

"She has been all week," Ethan said, trying his best to keep his calm. But, now that the two familiars had appeared, he was getting more and more anxious by the second. "Look, Eliza's in trouble and I have to help her. Are you coming or not?"

"I'm coming," Luke replied, though Ethan could hear the reluctance in his voice. Not to mention see it in the way the other man was standing. But working on Luke's opinion on Eliza would have to wait until after she was definitely safe.

"Lead on," Ethan said, turning to Flame and Bluebird. The two familiars stopped their frantic whizzing, and faced the same direction. They moved forward quickly, stopping every few moments to make sure the two witches were following. For whatever reason, the humans around them didn't seem aware of the two magic fuelled birds flitting around, which was making Ethan even more worried. Very few paranormals had the skill to make humans oblivious, and it wasn't one that was used often even by those who could. Unless they were up to no good. And considering Bluebird and Flame's behaviour, that wasn't a good sign.

It didn't take long for them to travel through the club, though to Ethan it felt like an age. His every thought was focused on Eliza, and the danger that she was probably in. No longer caring who he risked revealing himself to, he summoned magic and his hands crackled with red sparks. Beside him, Luke followed suit, his own more orange sparks, lighting around his tightly clenched fists. No matter what he might have to say about Eliza, Ethan knew that Luke had his back.

The two familiars led them to a scruffy door, clearly one not meant to be seen by the general public. Ethan pushed it open without hesitation, too caught up in the potential ideas of what he might find on the other side. The two witches stepped into a dingy alley, filled with a pregnant silence and nothing else.

Ethan created a ball of light between his hands, and sent it into the air in front of him. The red tinge like that tainted all of his magic, made the alley glow unnaturally. But the benefits of being able to see where he was going, far outweighed the eerie lighting.

Flame and Bluebird had disappeared from sight, making Ethan think that, despite the unnatural silence, there was someone about. Taking a step forward, he followed his gut instinct, growing more concerned by the second about what he was going to find. He turned a corner, with Luke hot on his heels, to find Eliza being held in place by a closely shaved thug, and a second man speaking close to her face. She was putting on a brave face, but Ethan could see the fear in her eyes, even from this distance.

"Have you heard what they say about witch blood, Gunter?" The thug shook his head and Ethan's heart sank as his suspicions were confirmed; the men that had Eliza were vampires, and the slighter of the two was likely to be fairly old and powerful. Things weren't looking good. "Apparently, the magic in their blood gives a buzz like no other. I can't wait to find out." The man moved forward and Eliza whimpered, but didn't scream.

Not wanting to startle any of them, Ethan slowly crept forward, cocking his head at Luke to go to the other side. He didn't doubt that Eliza had tried to use magic to get free, but it seemed like that hadn't worked. However, this time, there'd be three of them using magic. Not to mention Ethan's determination to save the woman he loved. He wouldn't fool himself into thinking that he was the strongest witch about, but he had something to fight for, and that would make all the difference.

He extinguished the ball of light, not wanting to tip off the two vampires that they were there. Though neither of them had even looked up at their approach; they were too engrossed in their plans for Eliza.

Ethan's heart was pounding, and his throat went dry. Too much was riding on the next few minutes, and that was what was keeping him going. It took a few moments, but when Eliza's frightened eyes locked on his, he saw relief flood over her face, quickly followed by determination.

Unnoticed by the two vampires, Eliza's hands began to spark blue, and Ethan's magic rose to join it. If he still doubted that they were meant to be together, then the multi-hued sparks covering his hands would have changed his mind. He'd never seen anything like it, even his parents' magic hadn't combined like this. Not taking his eyes off Eliza, not even to check that Luke was in position, he readied himself.

Without warning, she head-butted the vampire in front of her, the shock of it making him reel back, despite the fact that he was no doubt much stronger than she was. Ethan rushed forward, desperate to help her get free of the thug. But Eliza had other ideas, and stamped her heel down on the instep of the man behind her, causing his grip to loosen and Eliza to wriggle free a little. She lifted her magic covered hand to the thug's chest. Pressing down, she sent a shock through him at the same time Luke attacked.

The thug collapsed before their eyes, the combined magic of two witches being too much for him. Unfortunately, it also seemed to be too much for the pair of them, and Ethan had to watch as his best friend, and the love of his life, collapsed into a heap.

He rushed forward, completely forgetting about the other vampire until his path was blocked. The vampire sneered, before lunging at Ethan. He ducked just in time, narrowly avoiding a punch to his face. While Ethan went to the gym pretty regularly, he wasn't exactly trained to be in a fight. If he survived this situation in one piece, then that was definitely something he was going to rectify. Maybe it was something that Eliza would do with him.

"Hey! You alright, mate?" A slurred voice shouted from the edge of the alley, causing both Ethan and the vampire to look towards the man. Ethan wanted to shout at the man to run away, but the vampire was quicker, his eyes flaring red and a hiss escaping his mouth. He lurched towards the man and it took Ethan a moment to realise what was happening. While all he wanted to do was check on Eliza, he knew that he couldn't leave the poor man to the mercy of an angry vampire, even if it meant putting himself back into danger.

In the few seconds it had taken him to decide, the vampire had reached the man, and bitten down on his neck, choking off a scream. Ethan reacted, but was pushed out of the way by a tall woman with shockingly pink hair.

"I'll deal with it," she muttered, followed by something that sounded suspiciously like, "bloody witches."

Ethan watched as she strode up to the vampire and lifted him off the poor man with ease. She held him by his neck and slammed him against the wall, a menacing look in her eyes.

"Eden," the male vampire managed to choke out, despite the fact that she must be crushing his windpipe. Which confirmed Ethan's suspicion that vampires didn't actually need to breathe.

"I thought we'd told you to stop, Todd?" Ethan frowned, unsure what to make of the fact that the vampire's name was so ordinary. It just seemed wrong. "I should finish you right now," she growled, teeth descending from her mouth.

"You can't do that without the Council's permission," Todd stuttered, his face revealing to Ethan that he really wasn't sure about whether that would happen. The pink-haired vampire laughed, leaving Ethan with a slightly uneasy feeling about what he was witnessing. He'd heard rumours that the Vampire Council tended to be ruthless when one of their kind went off the rails.

"And give you time to talk to Maurice again? Not a chance." She withdrew something from her long dark coat, but Ethan was distracted by a moan coming from nearby. He turned back to where Eliza and Luke were, glad to see that Luke, at least, seemed fully conscious again, though he was rubbing his forehead as if it was paining him. Eliza's eyes were still closed, though he could see her chest rising and falling, and breathed a sigh of relief. Collapsing beside her, he scooped her into his arms, artfully ignoring the sounds coming from down the alley.

"Is he dead?" he asked slowly, feeling slightly sick at the thought that he had something to do with it. Even if they'd had no other choice. Luke shuffled over to where the thug was lying, gingerly checking his pulse before pulling his hand away and frowning.

"How do you even know if a vampire's dead?" Luke asked. Ethan shrugged, not quite sure how they managed to get involved in this situation in the first place. Up until now, the only paranormals he'd met, apart from his family, were Luke and Eliza.

"Only way of knowing for sure, is to stab one through the heart." Both Luke and Ethan turned to look at the pink-haired vampire, who was now standing over them, a serious look on her face and a drop of blood at the corner of her mouth. Ethan didn't want to think about where it had come from. "Decapitation works just as well, but it's much messier," she added after a few moments of silence.

"Do you have something to stab him with?" Luke asked, plenty of hesitation in his voice. Ethan imagined that his friend was feeling much as he did; a little disgusted, but knowing that it was for the best. The vampire frowned.

"I'll do it. Just get her out of here." She nodded at Eliza, who was still unconscious in Ethan's arms.

"What about the human?" Ethan asked, slowly staggering to his feet, doing his best to hold Eliza steady. To his surprise, Luke jumped to his feet, and helped him support her.

"It's too late for him," she said sadly and glanced back at where the man was lying. He wasn't moving at all, and there was a small pool of blood near his neck. "You need to be gone before he wakes up, there's never any telling how a new vampire will act."

"You turned him?" Luke asked. Ethan couldn't decide whether his friend was disgusted or just shocked.

"Considering the other option was letting him die, then yes. I turned him," she snapped back, clearly annoyed at the situation.

"Ethan?" Eliza's weak voice broke through the tension, and the three of them looked at her.

"Hey, Liza. It's all okay now," he soothed, placing a gentle kiss on her forehead.

"What happened?" she asked, blinking rapidly, not fully aware of where she was yet.

"I'll explain later, we need to get you home and safe first." She nodded, and snuggled into him, surprising him. Eliza had never been one for admitting weakness, and that showed how taxing the experience had been for her. "Thank you," he said to the other woman. He wasn't sure what would've happened if she hadn't shown up when she had.

"Don't mention it," she waved it off. "But, I'd ask that you keep what happened tonight to yourselves, it'll cause all kinds of trouble if you don't." Ethan nodded. He didn't need to be told twice. He didn't like to think about the kind of things that could happen to him if the vampires got involved.

CHAPTER ELEVEN

Eliza felt like she'd spent all night drinking, and then a brass band had then moved in next door. She blinked a few times, trying to work out exactly what had happened last night, but as far as she could remember, she'd only had two drinks. And she'd not even finished the second one when she'd run into Todd. There was something odd about the run-in, but she couldn't quite put her finger on what.

"Morning, Liza. How're you feeling today?" A gentle hand stroked her hair, smoothing it away from her face and making her feel a lot calmer.

"Ethan?" She was fairly certain that it was Ethan who was with her, but that raised as many questions as it answered. She hadn't even known that he was in the same club last night.

It was then that the events of the night came

flooding back to her. She sat bolt upright, sending a wave of dizziness through her, and Ethan to begin fussing.

"Liza, you need to lie down. You did a lot of magic last night, it took a lot out of you." He pushed her back down, and she didn't resist.

"Is Delilah alright? The other people? And what magic did I do?" She frowned in confusion, hating all the questions that she didn't have answers for.

"They're all fine, Delilah texted you this morning. I know I shouldn't have read it, but I wanted her to know that you were okay. I don't think they remember anything." He handed her phone to her, with the text screen open at the message stream from Delilah. She scanned the messages, and was relieved to see that, as far as the others were concerned, they'd just had a crazy night and couldn't remember some of it. She also saw Ethan's reply, which he'd signed as himself, telling Delilah that they'd run into each other unexpectedly and she'd gone back with him. She knew she should be mad at him for doing it without her permission, but she just couldn't summon the emotion; she'd clearly been in trouble last night, and he'd clearly saved her. She didn't really have the grounds to be mad at him.

"And the magic?"

Ethan looked unsure, but raised his hand

between them, a look of concentration on his face. She watched in awe as the sparks lit around his fingers. Instead of the red sparks that normally came from him, they were mixed with blue sparks like hers. Hesitantly, Eliza lifted her own hand and summoned magic, not sure what she was expecting. Like Ethan's, her hand was covered in a mixture of blue and red sparks.

"How?" she asked in awe.

"I've no idea, I've never heard of anything like it." He shrugged. "Luke's seeing if he can find out anything for us," he added, a nervous look on his face.

"Luke from school?" She shifted uncomfortably. They'd got on well until she'd started to date Ethan. After that, it had been as if he couldn't stand being in the same room as her. Ethan nodded.

"He was there last night," Ethan said. Eliza had a brief recollection of someone helping her take down the thug. That must have been Luke.

"What about Bluebird and Flame? Are they okay?" she asked, frantically looking around the room for them. Every morning since she'd started seeing Ethan again, the two familiars had always been around when she'd woken up.

"They're about somewhere. And they're their normal colours too. It's just our magic itself that's acting weird. But, how can I complain, when it's just more proof that we should be together."

She smiled at that, loving how affectionate Ethan was. He'd been that way for as long as she could remember, but it meant so much more now they were older. She still didn't quite understand what was going on with that. Hopefully Luke would have some answers for them soon, but she'd do some digging of her own at some point.

"So, I take it you have nowhere to be today," she said with a wink. Lying back down had cleared the dizzy feeling, and she was feeling a lot better already.

"Not unless you do."

"Good." She propped herself up, and reached out for him, pulling him down onto the bed. Ethan perched over her, his toned physique taking her breath away. She still wasn't used to his new look. Not that she was complaining. She trailed her hand down his chest, grateful that he hadn't felt the need to cover up with a shirt. And that the shirt he wasn't wearing, was all that she was.

"Are you sure, Liza? Last night took a lot out of you, I understand if you're not up to it." He kissed her cheek softly, but Eliza was having none of it, and trailed her hand further done, pushing it beneath the elastic of his boxers.

"More than sure." She smiled up at him, and a surge of satisfaction went through her as his breath caught and his face flushed with pleasure. She leaned in and nipped his neck playfully. Ethan groaned, and she released him, using magic to make their clothes and the bed sheet disappear; times like this, she loved being a witch.

"Liza, I'm not going to be able to wait long," he said through baited breath.

"Fine by me," she panted back, taking him in her hand and guiding him into her. She arched her back and let out a long satisfied moan. There was something about being together with him that put the rest of her experiences to shame. He was her one, and moments like this made that crystal clear.

EPILOGUE

TEN YEARS LATER...

ETHAN WALKED through the door of their suburban home, smiling to himself as he looked at the newly painted blue front door, and the window boxes that Eliza had been tending to since they'd moved in four years ago. Up until then, she hadn't realised that she had such a gift for it, and as it had coincided with her starting maternity leave, she'd started her own plant nursery in the greenhouse at the back. Once the twins had been born, the two of them had talked it through, and decided that she should concentrate on that instead of going back to work.

"Gemma, don't do that," he heard his wife say, and he wondered what his daughter was doing now. He turned into the living room to find his dark-haired twins giggling in the corner, and their poor cat hiding behind the sofa. Eliza stood in the doorway, mixing something in a bowl. Purple sparks came to life by the cat, making it hiss and slink further back behind the sofa. Ethan strode over to his children and scooped them both up in his arms.

"Gemma, don't do that," he said sternly, though secretly he was kind of proud of her. He'd pulled very similar pranks when he was her age.

"Daddy, it was Derrick," she said in her childlike voice, slurring her rs so that they sounded like ws.

"Gemma," he drew out her name. "Your brother can't do magic yet, we know it was you." She giggled slightly as she tried to look sorry.

"Sorry, Daddy."

"And?"

"Sorry, Mummy." Eliza smiled and came over to the three of them, after setting down her mixing bowl. She took Gemma from him, allowing Ethan to slip his arm around her waist and draw her to him. She rested her head on his shoulder, making Ethan feel like the luckiest man in the world. Sure, there were still some mysteries in their lives; namely that they still had no idea what happened with their magic that night, but every time he used it, it made him smile to know just how destined they were.

Mysteries aside, he had a beautiful wife, and two children he adored. And with them, he had everything that he'd ever needed.

The End

Thank you for reading *The Familiar's Wings*. If you'd like more paranormal romance, why not try the first book in the *MatchMater Paranormal Dating App* series, *Reluctant Dragon Mate*: http://books2read.com/reluctantdragonmate

Reluctant Dragon Mate is the first book in the MatchMater Paranormal Dating App series, which follows paranormals as they find their mates using a dating app! You can find it here: http://books2read.com/reluctantdragonmate

* * *

DAKOTA

DON'T MAKE important life decisions while drunk.

It was the mantra Dakota had lived her life by. Well, if she was honest, she just avoided getting drunk very often, which was fairly easy as a witch. But tonight was different. Tonight she'd been stood up.

She kicked off her heels and flopped down on her bed, dropping her clutch bag beside her. It hardly even mattered where it landed, so long as it was in reach.

She pulled out her phone and searched for the MatchMater app. She'd promised herself she wouldn't use it again, not after the string of disastrous dates she'd had over the past couple of months, but considering the no show of her current date, it was better this than nothing.

A vampire. A wolf shifter. An elf. She swiped left on them all for one reason or another. It was almost like something was spurring her on that didn't normally. And she liked it.

Her fingers finally came to rest when a dragon shifter with a mischievous grin and dishevelled black hair caught her eye. He looked like he'd just gotten out of bed. Definitely not her type, and yet there was a strong urge to swipe right even if she knew she shouldn't.

Before she could chicken out, she did it, only to be greeted by an obnoxious array of hearts that always happened when two people matched together.

That she hadn't expected. She didn't think she was anything special. Pretty enough without being drop-dead gorgeous, and just a completely run of the mill witch.

Hi. The message popped up via MatchMater's in-app messaging service.

She sucked in a breath. Had he really responded that quickly?

Hey, she typed back before deleting and retyping it twice. It seemed like both too much and too little at the same time. Maybe this was why she didn't have any luck when it came to the app, she just didn't know how to properly interact with men, especially not paranormal ones.

Hey, she eventually sent.

What are you doing up this time of night?

At least he was typing in full. She'd gotten rid of many suitors for text talk. She just couldn't stand it.

I've been out, she responded.

With friends?

On a date. There was no point lying about how badly it had gone.

Ouch. Must have been a lousy lay.

Dakota snorted and shifted on the bed so she could lean on her side.

He didn't show at all, she admitted.

For a beautiful woman like you?

Maybe all of my photos are fake. A smile twisted on her lips. She was enjoying this more than she thought possible, though maybe it was just because she was still a little drunk.

How would he know that if he didn't come to see you? The man asked. She really should check what his name was, but it almost didn't matter. Just the way he was talking to her was flattering enough and was certainly what she needed after the awful lack of date.

You have a point.

So why aren't you mated yet?

That's very forward. Her thumb hovered over the send button. Did she dare say the one thing that might end their conversation? Then again, this man wasn't the kind she'd be spending the rest of her life with. He'd be good for a bit of flirting and perhaps a quick tumble between the sheets and nothing more. She hit the button. If he stopped talking to her then she'd just shut off the light and go to sleep, no harm done.

Perhaps, but I don't want to get caught up in any jealous mate situations.

Has that happened before? She almost tripped over her fingers in her haste to type. She was desperate to learn more about this man and his experiences.

You'd be surprised what I've seen.

Finally giving in to her curiosity, she pressed his profile picture to find out his name. Achilles. It oddly suited the man she could see in the picture, especially as a dragon shifter. One of the advantages of MatchMater was that, not only was everyone on there a paranormal, but they all went through the same screening process to assure they were who they said they were. It sometimes surprised her just how many users there were because of the strict profile policies. But then, in this day and age, it was difficult enough to find a mate. This was just an easy way of taking advantage of modern technology.

Tell me...

Maybe if we were in person, he responded.

Do you want to make that happen? In the morning, she'd blame the alcohol for her boldness.

Now who is being forward?

Maybe I just know what I want. A confidence she rarely felt surged through her. Could she really do this? Could she invite him back to her place? All she wanted was to feel good, and he didn't need to be her mate for her to take that.

I like that in a woman.

Why don't you show me how much...

I'm starting to think you're nothing but a tease.

She bit her lip. She wasn't completely sure she wanted him to turn up at her door, but something deep within her tugged on her, urging her to say yes.

Why don't you come find out? Her thumb hovered

over the send button as the two sides warred within her. She'd never been the most impulsive person. Then again, that had just gotten her a string of disappointing dates and no mate. She had her career at least, but that was a small solace during the lonely nights.

Knowing she'd probably regret not sending the message more than she would letting the choice slip by, she hit send.

Nerves fluttered in her stomach as she waited for the reply. What if it was too much, too soon?

Send me your address.

Dakota sighed in relief and typed it out, hitting send immediately.

She hoped she wouldn't come to regret this. Or that he wouldn't show up at all. She'd taken quite enough rejection for one week and didn't intend to endure more unless she absolutely had to. Finding her mate was supposed to be easier in this day and age, especially since the Councils started to accept that different kinds of paranormals could be fated mates.

And yet, she wasn't finding it easier at all. Far from it. No matter where she looked, she kept finding men who just wanted a tumble in the sheets and nothing more. So now, she was going to do exactly that. There was no shame in it. She'd tried human men for a while but had found it impossible to let go completely in case her sparks flew and revealed the truth about her. She was certain a lot of people wouldn't believe that witches existed, but just one was enough.

A nudge at her leg drew her attention to the tiny dragon made of sparks nestled next to her.

"Okay, Rhi, a couple of pets, but then you have to go." She leaned down to scratch the creature's head, knowing it would disappear the moment Achilles came near her home. That was just how familiars worked. Only the witch they belonged to would be able to see them. Though she'd heard whispers that a witch's mate could also see them. She had no proof of that though. She was just going to have to wait and see on that front. And hope whoever it was she was destined for wouldn't take too long to appear.

Get Reluctant Dragon Mate here: http:// books2read.com/reluctantdragonmate

Books in the Paranormal Council Universe

- The Paranormal Council Series (shifter romance, completed series)
- The Fae Queen Of Winter Trilogy (paranormal/fantasy)
- Spring Fae Duology (paranormal/fantasy)
- Thornheart Coven Series (witch romance)
- Return Of The Fae Series (paranormal post-apocalyptic, completed series)
- Paranormal Criminal Investigations Series (urban fantasy mystery)
- MatchMater Paranormal Dating App Series (paranormal romance, completed series)
- The Necromancer Council Trilogy (urban fantasy)
- Standalone Stories From the Paranormal Council Universe

Books in the Obscure World

- Ashryn Barker Trilogy (urban fantasy,

completed series)
- Grimalkin Academy: Kittens Series (paranormal academy, completed series)
- Grimalkin Academy: Catacombs Trilogy (paranormal academy, completed series)
- City Of Blood Trilogy (urban fantasy)
- Grimalkin Academy: Stakes Trilogy (paranormal academy)
- The Harpy Bounty Hunter Trilogy (urban fantasy)
- Bite Of The Past (paranormal romance)
- Sabre Woods Academy (paranormal academy)
- The Shadow Seer Association (urban fantasy)

Books in the Forgotten Gods World

- The Queen of Gods Trilogy (paranormal/mythology romance)
- Forgotten Gods Series (paranormal/mythology romance, completed series)

The Grimm World

- Grimm Academy Series (fairy tale

academy)
- Fate Of The Crown Duology (Arthurian Academy)
- Once Upon An Academy Series (Fairy Tale Academy)

Other Series

- Untold Tales Series (urban fantasy fairy tales)
- The Dragon Duels Trilogy (urban fantasy dystopia)
- ME Contemporary Standalones (contemporary romance)
- Standalones
- Seven Wardens, co-written with Skye MacKinnon (paranormal/fantasy romance, completed series)
- The Firehouse Feline, co-written with Lacey Carter Andersen & L.A. Boruff (paranormal/urban fantasy romance)
- Kingdom Of Fairytales Snow White, co-written with J.A. Armitage (fantasy fairy tale)

Twin Souls Universe

- Twin Souls Trilogy, co-written with Arizona Tape (paranormal romance, completed series)
- Dragon Soul Series, co-written with Arizona Tape (paranormal romance, completed series)
- The Renegade Dragons Trilogy, co-written with Arizona Tape (paranormal romance, completed series)
- The Vampire Detective Trilogy, co-written with Arizona Tape (urban fantasy mystery, completed series)
- Amethyst's Wand Shop Mysteries Series, co-written with Arizona Tape (urban fantasy)

Mountain Shifters Universe

- Valentine Pride Trilogy, co-written with L.A. Boruff (paranormal shifter romance, completed series)
- Magic and Metaphysics Academy Trilogy, co-written with L.A. Boruff (paranormal academy, completed series)
- Mountain Shifters Standalones, co-written with L.A. Boruff (paranormal romance)

Audiobooks: www.authorlauragreenwood.co.
uk/p/audio.html

Laura is a USA Today Bestselling Author of paranormal and fantasy romance. When she's not writing, she can be found drinking ridiculous amounts of tea, trying to resist French Macaroons, and watching the Pitch Perfect trilogy for the hundredth time (at least!)

FOLLOW THE AUTHOR

- Website: www.authorlauragreenwood. co.uk
- Mailing List: www. authorlauragreenwood.co.uk/p/mailing-list-sign-up.html
- Facebook Group: http://facebook.com/ groups/theparanormalcouncil
- Facebook Page: http:// facebook.com/authorlauragreenwood
- Bookbub: www.bookbub.com/authors/ laura-greenwood

- Instagram: www. instagram.com/authorlauragreenwood
- Twitter: www.twitter.com/lauramg_tdir

Printed in Great Britain
by Amazon